ZAK RAVEN
CODE ALPHA

Darren G. Davis

FIRST PRINTING, November 2018.
Harry Markos, Director.

Paperback: ISBN 978-1-912700-35-6
eBook: ISBN 978-1-912700-36-3

Written and created by Darren G. Davis

Copy Editor: Diana Swartz
Assistant Editor: Emma Davis
Cover illustration by Sean Murphy and Blond

Book design by: Ian Sharman

www.markosia.com

First Edition

This book is dedicated to the person in my life who has made my life an adventure.
Thanks, Diana!

This book would not be possible without the following people: Jason Schultz, Zach Hunchar, Debbie Bishop, Steve Montal, Emma Davis, Ciara Sarver and Martha Davis.

ALSO PUBLISHED BY
MARKOSIA

THE THRONE ETERNAL

DORIAN GRAY

SINBAD: ROGUE OF MARS

SWANSONG

WORDS ON A WALL

PROLOGUE

Where do I begin? I guess I should start by telling you who I am. My name is Zak Raven, and I am from a small town in Southern California called Bluffside. It's not the biggest town in the world, but it's home. Bluffside is small, the kind of town where everyone knows everyone else's business. There are block parties, church socials and everyone turns out to support the high school football team. Trick-or-treating is still an event. It's a great place to grow up.

October is my favorite time of year. The weather starts to get cold, though by Southern California standards the coolest night is around fifty degrees. Last winter break we had a heat wave and I never got out of shorts. It's kinda weird that my family back east is shoveling snow from their walkways while I'm getting a tan. Sometimes I wish I was someplace that has real seasons. Last year, on vacation in the fall, my aunt took me to Seattle and I got to see the leaves change color. It was amazing, but I could do without all the rain. Sometimes I run on about things, so I will return to the story at hand.

I'm a freshman at Bluffside High, your average high school. All the cliques are there: the jocks, geeks, drama freaks and the wood shop people, who are a category all their own. Myself, I am the outsider. You would think I could identify with one of the thousand cliques at school, but people view me either as the town freak or its guardian. I guess I should fill you in on the reason for this.

As a young kid, I had superpowers along the lines of Superman. I had the speed and strength of a train; I could even fly…. Geez, how I miss the flying. I was the pride of the town. Not even the local football team would get as much press as I did. I still look back at the press clippings that my mom cut out on my "super" career. I would come to the rescue of villains trying to take over the world. At age ten, I would stop bank robberies. The only thing I did not get is why superheroes had to wear tights. Sure, they were easy to hide under your clothes, but they were really uncomfortable. You might think they'd be warm, but a night I would freeze my bottom off. The cape was cool, I have to say. There's nothing like the sound of a cape flapping in the breeze while you're flying around the city.

I've always felt like a square peg in a round hole. As much as the town admired me for the deeds that I did, it was hard to find people like myself to understand me. I met a couple of superheroes in a time when the world was in crisis, Judo Girl and the 10th Muse. We banded together and joined our powers to fight evil. We saved the world and formed the Society of Superheroes. Even though I was the youngest by ten years, it was great to have them to confide in and occasionally fight crime with. I still have a thing for Judo Girl!

Sometimes you have to laugh at some of the villains who made it to Bluffside. The Vermin – he tunneled into the sewers in an attempt at taking over the world. He infested a Bluffside monument, trapping twenty people in the town clock tower, and demanded twenty million dollars or he'd blow it to bits. Where do guys like the Vermin get these figures, anyway? Do they calculate in their heads how much they're in debt, then account for the cost of living? Why twenty million dollars? Why not forty million dollars or even one billion dollars? After a stand-off of more than three hours, the police let me go in and do my thing. Within five minutes I trapped the rat. Sometimes I don't understand the police.

The one person I still cannot catch with his hands dirty is the crime lord Genghis Cohen.

Then there was my favorite, the Rainbow Clown, not only did he hold up the bank with arsenic pies, he drove this goofy little car. I have to give him credit, though: He did mange to catch me with his balloon animals. Never underestimate the power of a balloon poodle. The problem with the old-school villains is they need to have some big plan to destroy you. I was caught in a giant, sand-filled hourglass with the sand running down. Of course the Rainbow Clown thought he had me and left to commit more crimes. What he didn't know is that I had a sonic glare that busted the glass. Oh, yeah. Twenty minutes later, he was behind bars.

As I got older, my powers faded. A fallen movie star with a couple of flop movies, I eventually became a has-been. High school was tough enough without being a freak. Then I was picked on more than others were because I was different.

The part that really bums me out is not the glory and fame but the fact that I was doing good and helping people. Batman had no real superpowers, right? This is a good place for the story to start.

CHAPTER ONE

Torrance Raine is the prettiest and popular girl in the ninth grade. Not only is she the head of the Junior Varsity cheerleading squad, but she is in every club on campus, from the Interact Club to the French Club. She is the reason kids want to study French instead of Spanish. She has long brown hair that flows off her shoulders, and she always smells of vanilla… OK, I'm getting off the subject again.

Bluffside is not a big town, and Torrance and I have attended the same schools since preschool. Now we have four out of six classes together. Our names follow each other on the attendance roster, which means that I usually sit behind her in classes. The only time I get to interact with her is when we are passing class papers up and down our row of desks. You can learn a lot about a person from seeing tests and homework passed to you. She has amazing penmanship, but I've noticed her grades have lowered since her mother passed away two years ago. Her father, Dimitri Raine, is the head chemist for the Epic Shampoo Company and raised Torrance alone after his wife died. Nobody knows the real story of how she died, but the talk around school was cancer. Her mother was the librarian at our elementary school, so I knew her well. I was always spending time in the library, studying my foes and learning how to defeat them. I would read about solvents that could combat meringue from toxic pies or how to capture vermin. Sometimes I would be there after school for hours just looking up stuff. Mrs. Raine would always go out of her way to help me and offer advice and cookies. She was a wonderful woman, which I think is part of the reason I like Torrance so much.

We are sitting in science class when Mr. Brady is taking attendance. Since the loss of my powers, science has become one of my favorite subjects. I'm hoping to find a way to get back my powers with the aid of modern science, but something tells me I won't learn it this week as we are learning about why cats have whiskers. Unless I turn into Catman, I am at a loss. But I did learn that if I trim my cat's whiskers he'd have a heck of a time navigating his way around in the dark. They work as antennae, enabling a cat to identify things he cannot see. My superpower would be nothing more than lazily lounging on a couch all day only to wake for food and an occasional pet from my owner. Some of the villains I've fought were so clueless, even a super-lazy power could bring them to justice.

My grandmother could capture some of those guys, especially the Clutter King. He had an army of tacky figurines trying to take over the local jewelry store. That night my grandmother was driving her car to the local grocery store, when the Clutter King ran out and she backed into him. She did not know that she had him pinned against the wall. Her hearing is pretty bad. When I flew down to see what all the commotion was about, there were ceramic figures trying to break him free. With a big superbreath and a wall, the figures were history. The Clutter King looked up at me just as the cops arrived. My grandmother was a hero. She was in the newspaper the next day. It must run in the family.

I am siting three chairs from Torrance. In Brady's class we get random seating, so she is sitting next to her friend Ciara Monet. I, on the other hand, am sitting next to Bad Body Odor Brian, who always smells really gross. Being the outsider of the school does not give one the option of sitting next to normal people. It makes it worse that he does not take a shower in gym class, which he has before this class.

All I can do is stare at Torrance, thinking about our life together. After college she is an accomplished author with her second bestseller and I am the head of a successful corporation. We have a big house in the country as well as homes in France, Italy and Big Bear, Calif. We have a bunch of dogs and horses. I always wanted horses. We play tennis on our tennis court. I'm usually better at the game then her, but I do let her win from time to time…

"Mr. Raven… Mr. Raven."

"Huh?"

"Are we keeping you up?" Mr. Brady asks, and the class starts laughing at me. I shrink down into my chair. "Um… Sorry, Mr. Brady," I say. Even Body Odor Brian is laughing.

Mr. Brady says, "Please see me after class." Snickers follow his words. I look back over to Torrance, who is not even fazed by the situation. Mr. Brady returns to his lecture on the animal kingdom. He is on a roll with the weight difference between an adult pot-bellied pig and a common farm pig. Ah, the fun of ninth-grade science class. Since we are learning about vertebrates, I should mention that his syllabus includes plans for us to dissect a frog. At least in tenth grade we move from the animal kingdom to subatomic particles.

After what seems like an eternity, the bell finally rings. The students gather their books and backpacks and head for the door. Colton Williams walks by my desk and kicks my books and calls me a freak. Colton is the biggest jerk in the ninth grade. He is sort of dating Torrance and I am guessing knows about my crush on her. This is why he is extra jerk-like to me. He is the big dumb jock type who has just learned that he is the Big Man on Campus. He moved here last year from some southern state. He's heard the stories of my days as a hero but sees me as the outsider I have become. So he can say he can beat up the "Kid Ranger" to his friends back home, I am guessing that this gives him more reason to pick on me. Three years ago I could have used my heat ray to burn his hair off, but those days are over. All I can do is sit back and wait twenty years, until I am a successful financier and he is fat and bald and working at the local convenience store. I would walk into his store, pay for my slushie with a thousand-dollar bill and pretend he does not exist. Then I'd jump into my Mercedes with Torrance in the passenger seat.

"MR RAVEN! Are you listening to me?" I start collecting the books that fell on the floor and put them into my backpack. "Umm… Huh? Oh… Sorry, Mr. Brady."

"I understand that you have a lot on your mind, but you need to pay attention to class. Do I have to remind you of your last test score?" Those words from Mr. Brady kinda stung.

So I got a C-minus on my last test. It's not like I am failing the course. When in my life will I ever need to know about photosynthesis or carbon dating? OK, maybe if a supervillain decided to steal our sunlight in order to kill all the plants, which filter our air. That would destroy all dependent beings, such as humans, animals and other plants. I would have to manufacture oxygen to save the day. Hmmm, I guess I am learning something in this class. Well, then why would carbon dating be important? The only dating I am concerned with is Torrance, and that is not going to happen anytime soon.

"Got it, Mr. Brady." I grab my backpack and head for the door.

"Mr. Raven, remember that we have a meeting after school. Please do not be late today."

"Understood, Chief." I stumble at the door, push it open hard and hear a thump from the other side. Now what?

Colton is cradling his arm in pain and mumbling something under his breath. His face starts to get really red, like the shade of a baboon's butt. This is not good.

He rushes at me and grabs me by my shirt. "Listen, freak, I have my eye on you," he says as I squirm to hold onto my backpack. It's no use. It opens and the books splatter onto the floor again. It seems that my books always end up on the floor when Colton's around.

"Colton! Let him go!" It was the voice of an angel.

"Come on, Torrance, the twit knocked into me," Colton whines.

"Let him go. You heard what Principal Montal said about you getting into another fight."

Colton drops me to the ground and I collect my books.

"Watch yourself, freak," he threatens and storms off, leaving me to my mess.

"This is yours." All I see is a hand holding my notebook.

As I look up at Torrance, I start to mouth "thanks," but our eyes meet and "Th... eeee... aaaaahmm" comes out instead. This is better than the last time I spoke to her and all I could muster was "Oo, pretty girl." I sounded like a caveman.

"I want to tell you he'll grow out of it, but let's face it, he won't," Torrance says. "Anyway, see you around." I can't do anything but watch her walk away.

"Good one, Zak." Another voice. My only real friend, Tyler, is walking toward me with a big, fat grin on his face. I am so flustered that I don't even acknowledge him.

Tyler is the only kid at school who I've known both before and after I had superpowers. Our mothers met in the maternity ward at St. Joseph's Hospital. Tyler and I were born only minutes apart from each other. He has always been my best friend and biggest supporter. In elementary school, he used to cover me when I had to fly off. Most of the teachers never knew that I had left the classroom. Having superpowers as a young kid has some advantages for your best friend. When we played with cars, we actually played with full-size automobiles. After a while, my parents' insurance was canceled because I kept slamming down the cars. You have to give me a break, though. I was six.

Tyler and I have remained friends all these years, and I know that we will be friends forever. He is tall and skinny and has a lot of potential. He has toyed around with the idea of becoming a firefighter, which I hope he does. It's a great way for him to be a hero, too. Most of the time he is really good in the face of danger. Then there are times when he runs at the site of a supervillain, but what normal person wouldn't?

Tyler waves his hands in front of my face. "Tyler to Zak. Come in, Zak" he spouts off.

"Huh? What? Oh, hey, Tyler."

"You are full of the 'huh-whats' today. You had the perfect opportunity to talk to her and you flubbed it."

"Thanks for all your love and support."

"Ha! That's what best friends are for…"

"You are a good sidekick, Tonto."

"Thank you, Kemosabe. So what's the deal-e-o for after school today? Wanna hit the Leaning Tower of Pizza?"

"Ugh. I can't. I have to train today with Mr. Excitement. You can come if you want."

"Geez, you were so much more fun when you had your powers, none of this stealth training stuff."

"Yeah, but now I get gadgets and a motorcycle."

"But you are not able to leap tall buildings in a single bound."

"Ah, but I have a grappling hook"

"You have a point. Can you get me one of those?"

"Not on your life! Remember the time you borrowed it to sneak into the drive-in? Most people sneak in by hiding in the trunk, but nooooo, not you. You had to do the cool, stealth-like thing. You shot the hook through the screen, and it looked liked Julia Roberts had a booger coming out of her nose. Then you just had to take it one step farther and push the release button and jet trough the screen."

"Come on, who wanted to see that movie anyway? Am I *still* paying that off?"

"Just meet me at the bike rack after school."

CHAPTER TWO

Torrance Raine's home is about a mile from my home and two blocks from Tyler's. I pass it all the time on my way to his house. Bluffside is known for all the homes looking similar to each other. It is the ultimate in suburban living. The houses are your basic two-story models, complete with white picket fences and perfectly manicured yards. Two-car garages and big backyards make Bluffside the perfect suburbia.

Roughly half of the homes have pools. Residents of the other half hang out at the homes of the pool people when the weather is unbearably hot. When the temperature gets to a hundred degrees, I'm practically living at Tyler's place.

At the end of Torrance's street is a state wildlife reserve. This is where I spend a lot of time hiking in the hills. Tyler and I used to ride our BMX bikes back there doing jumps and stuff. We would also go hiking for hours, looking for cool-shaped rocks and rose quartz. There was a time when we were little that Tyler's dad helped us build a fort in the hills out of wood. His father is a contractor, so there was never a shortage of wood for all the things we made. One night, Tyler and I camped out overnight in our fort. It was kinda creepy because we didn't realize that wildlife came out at night. Tyler would not let me sleep because of all the coyotes howling owls screeching. We never spent the night out there again.

The funny thing is that my fear of snakes never made an impact as we trudged though brush during the day. Superman has Kryptonite and my weakness is snakes. I am lucky that only Tyler knows about this, otherwise crime lords would use snakes instead of guns on me.

Nowadays, our BMX bikes collect dust in our garages. They have been traded in for mountain bikes.

"Welcome home, pumpkin," professor Raine calls out to Torrance from the kitchen.

"Thanks, Daddy." Torrance walks into the kitchen, where her father is drinking a smoothie and thumbing through the local paper. He's still wearing his lab coat. "I see that the circus is coming back to Bluffside. Your mother used to love the elephants, or was that you?"

"It was mom. She'd say they reminded her of your honeymoon in Africa."

"You are correct. Why don't I pick us up some tickets to the circus?"

"Dad, I'm too old for the circus."

"Humor your old man, will you?"

"OK, Daddy, if it means that much to you."

"Your mother would be proud of you. You are growing up so fast."

"Come on, Daddy. I will always be your little girl."

"How did you do on your English test?"

"Got a B."

"Without B's there would be no honey." He chuckles. "Can I make you a smoothie?"

"No, thanks. I have a bunch of homework to do."

"Are you sure, kitten? You know that smoothies are rich and nutritious."

"Maybe later." Torrance makes her way upstairs.

"Very well. I am going to do some work, too. Study like a bunny!"

Professor Raine finishes off his smoothie and heads outside. He looks up at Torrance's window and sees that she is already on the phone. Walking to the ten by ten shed in the backyard, he punches a five-digit code into the keypad on the door. The shed beeps but nothing happens. He punches in the code again and still nothing happens. Frustrated, he slaps the side of the shed and a doorway opens to a stairwell going down into darkness.

At the bottom of the stairs is another doorway. Once again, Raine taps a code into the keypad on the door and slips into an elevator that takes him two hundred feet below ground. There is elevator music in the background and Raine hums along with it.

The elevator door opens to a corridor. Raine walks the length of the hall and stops at the edge of a bottomless pit. There is a keyboard on the floor. Raine uses his feet to tap a four-digit code and a bridge slowly lowers from the ceiling to cover the pit. Still humming to the elevator music, he crosses the bridge and steps onto an escalator heading south. At the bottom of the escalator is pure blackness. He flips the light switch on the wall and the room lights up. He is in his laboratory. His eyes flutter as they turn solid gold and his skin takes on a silver tint. "Daddy's home!" he cries out.

CHAPTER THREE

I have had this locker for four months now and I still can't ever get it open on the first try.

"Zak, can I talk to you for a moment?" Principal Montal asks while I am trying to open my locker.

"Sure, Mr. Montal." I know this is not going to be good. The principal only talks to me when I am in trouble. He is not a big fan the superpowered types. This man makes more problems for me than anyone else in the school, so I try to stay out of his way as much as possible. Sometimes I feel like he has it in for me because his daughter stopped speaking to him after she married a superpower. He was quoted in the local papers as not accepting his daughter's marriage, and he even revealed her husband's secret identity.

Montal's revelation brought a lot of old villains out of the woodwork to seek out his son-in-law. His daughter and her husband joined the witness protection program and Montal hasn't seen his daughter since.

"We still have not spoken about last week's incident."

I knew this was coming. I try defending myself. "You see, I had no control over what happened."

"You blew up the boys' bathroom."

"I know. The doctors promised me it was the last time it could possibly happen. It was the last burst of energy that my body had from my superpowers. Seriously, you can call the Society of Superheroes. I'm normal now, just like you and her." I point to a random girl walking in the hall.

"You're anything but normal, Zak. I also know that you are still playing hero around town. I will not have any of this at my school. If it was up to me, you would not be at this school." He pauses. "If it was not for that darn school board you would not be here."

"Ouch." I look down. I know about his apprehensions of me coming here. My mother had to do a lot of work to convince the school board not to have me sent to a boarding school. Since Bluffside is a public school, they have to teach all kids, regardless of their differences or special needs. A letter from the president of the United States that helped convince the school board. Saving the president's daughter from the evil Binary Star has its benefits.

My mom and I were on a tour of the White House in Washington, D.C., a couple of years ago when the ground started shaking like an earthquake. Everyone on the tour ran out the double doors to the front lawn. I stayed behind to look around when someone ran into me and fell to the floor. It was the president's daughter. Just then a chandelier dropped from above. I covered her, and it crashed on top of me, shattering into a million pieces. We got up and were running out when the Binary Star appeared. I'd figured he was the one behind the earthquake. He shot a beam at us, not knowing that I was the Kid Ranger. I blocked it with my hand, sending it bouncing back into his face and blinding him. By this time, the Secret Service arrived and arrested him. For the rest of the trip, my mom and I got to dine with the president and stay in a room that many famous presidents stayed in. As for his daughter, we still stay in touch from time to time. That reminds me… I owe her a call.

Principal Montal barks at me one last time. "I have both eyes on you, Zak. If you even blink the wrong way, you will be out of this school."

I finally pop open my locker and toss my books into it.

CHAPTER FOUR

"Zak, can you ever be on time?" Tyler is sitting on the grass and looks annoyed as he taps his watch. He takes off his headphones. There are only a couple of bikes left in the bike rack besides mine.

"Sorry, my locker was stuck."

"You're a superhero. Couldn't you blast it or something?"

"Tyler, you know I told my parents that I wouldn't use any hero tricks at school. They want me to be a normal kid, and besides, I got pulled aside by our favorite principal." I pull out the calculator that Brady gave me and hit a couple of buttons on it. My ten-speed bike glows and shakes while it transforms into a supped-up motorcycle.

"Did he ask you to run for class president or for lunch in the teachers' lounge?"

"Hardly. I got the weekly warning not to blow up anything"

"That was so long ago. What, last month?"

"He just wishes he could kick me out of this school."

"Dude, you can't leave me. If you go, then I will have nobody to hang with at lunch."

"I'm not going anywhere, don't worry."

We put on our helmets and I start the motor. "Get on," I say, and Tyler jumps on the back of the bike and we drive off.

"I don't see what the big deal is," Tyler yells over the engine. "Everyone knows you had superpowers, but they're gone now, right? It's not like I am still scared of getting electric shocks. That one time you rubbed your feet on the carpet to shock me put me in the hospital!"

"I still feel bad about that."

"At least my mom will let me hang with you without supervision again since you lost your powers. But it kinda sucks that you had them and now you don't."

"Yeah, 'had' is the key word. Life was so much easier when I could do all these amazing things. I could fly, use superstrength, melt things with energy beams that came out of my hands…. I could make a difference. Now all I can do is train, train, train. I'm getting really sick of it."

"Nobody ever said the hero thing was going to be easy. You are the one who still wanted to fight crime once your powers went away. Didn't Mr. Brady tell you that your powers might come back?"

"He doesn't know for sure. Nobody does. All I want to do is help people."

"Come on, Zak, you help people all the time. You saved the mayor last month from the attack of evil bunnies."

"Hey, those giant rabbits were carrying rabies and multiplying every two minutes. Plus they had fleas. You were the one I had to save because you thought they were cute and fluffy. Then you got trapped in the giant carrot, and now I can't watch Bugs Bunny cartoons." I laugh.

"Geez, that carrot thing was bad. I am still trying to get the taste out of my mouth. Did you and Brady ever figure out who was behind it?"

"No, but he is working on it. I would help out more but he gave us that science project that I had to work on. My mom also grounded me for not doing my chores."

"You would think she would be cooler about the chores thing. You did manage to stop the rabbits from destroying your house."

"Yeah, but they left giant pellets on my mom's car, making it a convertible now. I will never hear the end of that one. Who knew that rabbit poop could crush the roof of a car?"

"Hahaha! Oh, Zak, your mom was so mad."

"Hold on. Something's coming over the police scanner."

I turn up the volume in my helmet and listen. "All available officers should be on the lookout for a blue sedan, license plate 345489W. Occupants are wanted for holding up Peachtree Auto Parts. Suspects were last seen at the corner of Westmont and Croft, heading south."

"Zak!" Tyler screams, "We just passed Westmont!"

"I know! Hold on!" I press the motorcycle's warp button and we jet down Smith Street. "I know a shortcut to head them off."

Tyler is holding on tight to me. I know he is scared. We're heading down Smith Street, toward the dead-end sign.

"Zak. Zak! ZAAAAAAK!"

I don't have time to drop him off. Tyler hates going on adventures with me. His mother used to get so mad at having to wash his clothes all the time because he would pee his pants. As mean as it sounds, I still laugh at that.

We are about a hundred feet from the dead end and traveling about seventy miles per hour toward a brick wall.

"ZAK!" Tyler screams again. I block out his screams and fix my eyes on a piece of wood in the road that if we hit wrong will send us flying into a wall. I have done this before but never with someone on the back of the bike. I have to calculate this factor into the jump. I need to go faster. We hit eighty mph and I hit the wood just right and we launch into the air. As we are soaring, the back tire just nicks the top of the wall. Tyler is crushing my ribs, but I need to concentrate on the landing. We hit the ground and wobble a bit. I can hear the tires screech on the cement below.

"Are we alive?" I can feel Tyler release his death grip on my ribs. "Please let me be alive. I still need to do things. If I come back dead, my mom is not going to forget it this time."

We are now beside the sedan. "Zak, there it is, the car." Tyler is pointing to it and I can sense that he is really scared. It's time to go solo.

"I see it. Stay here." I push a couple of buttons on the cycle.

"Stay here? Where would I go?" Tyler sounds confused.

I stand up on the seat of the motorcycle. I can feel Tyler's fear as I am doing this.

"Where are you going? Zak! Don't do this to me!"

He is still yelling, but I tune him out to concentrate on this move.

I leap into the air and hit the autopilot button on my wrist communicator for the motorcycle. An inflatable driver expands in the place on the motorcycle where I was sitting. Fully inflated Tyler grabs onto him and holds tightly.

I land on the hood of the blue sedan. Holding on, all I can think about is how much easier it would be if I still was able to fly. This would be a cakewalk. The car swerves to shake me off the hood. My grip slips so I use the suction cups on my gloves to hold on. I crawl up the hood to get a look at the driver. Just my luck, the windows are blacked out. All I can see is a blinking light inside, which starts blinking faster.

A beam of light shoots through the window, grazing my arm. I let go of the one of the suction cups and grab my shoulder. "That's going to leave a mark," I think as the pain sets in. I need to focus on the mission and not the pain. I suction back to the hood of the car.

I didn't know sedans came with a killing beam as an option. Another beam shoots through the window and misses me. I can see Tyler on the motorcycle peel away onto the sidewalk. Good thing no one is outside shopping right now. I had to open my mouth. There is a man sweeping the sidewalk in front of his store. He does not see Tyler coming. Tyler rides off the sidewalk, back onto the street and right next to the blue sedan. The dirt pile the man was sweeping into is blown all over the place. I can here him yelling in the background.

Tyler is racing beside the blue car. I tell the automatic pilot to pull back. I do not want Tyler getting hurt by the beams. I have to get this car to stop because someone can get hurt, namely me.

"OK, buster!" Did I just use the word "buster"? I press a button on my communicator that sends out a supersonic squeal to blow out the windshield. Glass sprays everywhere and my ears ring from the blast. I look into the car to see who is behind this. No one. The car is full of all these mechanical things but no people.

All of a sudden I feel the hood coming loose while I am still suctioned to it. The hood flips up, detaches from the car and I am airborne again. The hood is spinning and making me dizzy. I have only a few seconds to control it and make sure I land right. I use all my might to stop the spinning, then I hit the ground hard and start to skid.

"Just like a snowboard!" I scream out as if I am trying to make myself believe it.

A bunch of onlookers watch in amazement as I skid past them. There's a police car parked about hundred feet ahead, and the hood and I aren't slowing down. "This will give new meaning to the phrase 'protect and serve,'"

I think as I lean to the right and brace myself for the inevitable. SMASH!

The force of the impact releases my suction grip, and I tumble over the police car into a newspaper stand. A flurry of papers fills the air. People gather around to see if I am all right. I'm in some serious pain and lying in a pile of splintered wood and magazines, lots of magazines. I pull a magazine off my face. There's a figure looking over me.

"Mr. Raven… We spoke about your hero antics before. You are going to get yourself killed."

"Oh, hey, Officer Dent. I didn't notice you." I stumble to my feet. My head feels like it's been hit by a truck, and Officer Dent's words seem to go on forever. All I can do is stand there and take it.

After what seems like an hours-long lecture on my hero antics, my motorcycle pulls up with Tyler. He looks green. "Officer Dent, my ride is here. Once again, I am really sorry about your car."

"Just be careful," Dent warns me.

A man approaches Officer Dent, yelling something about his newsstand. Time to go.

I release the autopilot and it deflates back into the cycle. As I get back on the cycle, Tyler gets off. "I'm taking the bus," he tells me.

"Are you sure?" I laugh.

"Yeah, public transportation seems a bit safer than riding with you." Tyler heads for the bus stop and I drive off.

CHAPTER FIVE

I get to Brady's house and knock on the front door. As I'm waiting for someone to answer, I can't help but think about his wife. Brady really does not talk about her much. He's not a very personable kind of guy.

I met Mrs. Brady a couple of times. She thinks her husband is my science tutor and not my trainer hired by the Society of Superheroes.

Brady doesn't talk about his past much – and he won't explain how he got involved with the Society of Superheroes. All I know is he has top clearance with them. Personally, I've never seen any sign of superpowers in Brady, unless being a one-dimensional bore qualifies as a superpower.

Most of my contact with the Society has been revoked, but since I saved the world on more than one occasion, they are sort of indebted to train me. It's pretty pathetic when your parents have to sign a release form to be a superhero. I fought with some of the coolest heroes in the business: the 10th Muse, Trident and Atlas. But my favorite by far is Judo Girl. She was always so cool to me and treated me like an equal rather than a kid.

The Society of Superheroes is a nonprofit organization with the motto "There is never a time for crime." Kinda corny, but they do a lot good. The group has a revolving membership that seems to change with the season. I was only a junior member for a couple of years before I lost my powers. They had to cut me from the roster when my powers started to fade. It's really awkward when you are flying with someone in your arms and suddenly your ability to fly cuts out. Crashing into a parked car is a bad thing, and the Society's insurance went up with every crash I made. Fortunately, no one ever got hurt. I usually used my body as a shield during impact. Of course, that meant I got pretty beat up in the process, which starting causing problems with my judgment. I always depended on my powers for fighting, and I never got around to learning how to fight without them. This is where Brady stepped in — to teach me to use my senses and brain rather than rely on my brawn.

There is no answer at the door, so I walk around the back to his garage. I press the intercom button on the garage and wait for an answer.

"Hello?"

"Hey, it's me."

The garage door opens and it looks like a basic garage full of old furniture, boxes and oil stains on the floor. I walk toward the back and walk through the hologram wall. Now it is a sterile environment full of gadgets and test tubes. It is probably the coolest laboratory I've seen. I walk over to Brady, who's working on some object.

"Mr. Raven, you're late." He scowls at me.

"I know, but I have a good explanation for it."

"You always do."

"There was this car that…." He cuts me off. "I have someone I would like you to meet."

"You got me a football. Come on, Brady, you know that football is not my sport of choice. I'm more of a hockey person."

"This is your new… for lack of better words, your sidekick."

"Thanks Brady, but I am more of the Lone Ranger type. You know, solo artist."

"Are you finished?"

"Yeah. Um, sorry. So, what does this football thingy do?"

"This football thingy is a Laser-Enhanced Organic Robot. You can call him LEO."

"I know I got a B in English, but shouldn't it be LEOR?"

"We don't talk about the R," he snaps.

"Why not?" I press.

"Let's just say the R is silent." He is still fiddling with the robot and not looking at me.

"Well, that doesn't make sense. If the R was silent…"

"ZAK!"

"LEO? Couldn't you come up with anything cooler, like Robo-Tron? Even C-3PO sounds cooler than LEO.

"Zak it is an acronym. You know what that is, don't you?"

"Geez, that was harsh." I settle onto a stool.

"I'm glad I have your attention now."

"Did you make the robot?"

"It was donated by the Superhero Society. He is a device that can execute a wide range of maneuvers under the direction of a computer, which is held at the Superhero Society. Reacting to feedback from its sensors, a robot can alter its maneuvers to fit a changed task. He was used in threatening situations that the other members could not handle. The Society does not need him anymore, so they gave him to you."

"I get a used robot?"

Brady ignores my last comment and tells me about my new sidekick, using all sorts of boring scientific jargon.

"LEO is the ultimate weapon. Its light amplification system is comprised of synthetic radiation particles which synthesize monochromatic infrared beams. He will emit a light source…"

I just sit there with a blank look on my face as he babbles away. He's so excited to talk about this, so I let him go on. "Its projectiles can be expelled by the force of its jet propulsion, and it carries its own propellants and oxidizers."

Drool starts dribbling down the side of my face and I have to say something.

"Hey, Einstein. English, please. You're losing me."

"I forgot who my audience is. Sorry, Zak. It's a robot that has a lot of cool gadgets to help you stay out of trouble."

"How much does my baby-sitter make an hour?"

"Without your powers, you need the extra guidance, so please read the manual." He hands me this thick book full of big words and pictures.

"I have homework in my superhero life, too. Oh, great."

"It would be in your best interest to learn all about him, he is not a toy," he says in a very fatherly voice. Next thing I know, he'll be asking me to do is rake his leaves and take out the trash.

Brady is one of the only adult male figures in my life since my father died when I was two. I don't remember my father, so I rely on stories my mother tells me about him. He died of cancer when he was just thirty two. Mom says I was the light in his eyes.

He and my mother were high school sweethearts in Bridgeport, which is about sixty miles north of Bluffside. They married after graduating from college. My father got a job straight out of school, working as an accountant for a computer company in Bluffside. My mother was happy to move to this small community and work for the local veterinarian. A couple of years into their marriage, I was born and my mother gave up her career to stay home with me. Mom shared with me her love for animals, but

I didn't share my father's love for math. What I did get from my father is that I look exactly like him when he was my age.

My mother has a done a great job raising me. Once my father passed away, she went back to work part time as a veterinarian's assistant and now is going back to school to become one. I have always been close to her and she is my biggest supporter. She still clips articles on my heroics and me. She always tells me that my father would have been proud of me. I wish that I got to know him more than stories and pictures from my mother and grandparents.

CHAPTER SIX

I finally make it home with LEO. My neighbor Madison Kruse is sitting on his stoop, looking like he just lost his best friend. Madison is a ten-year-old kid who has been my biggest fan since the beginning. His room has posters of me in my superhero costume. It's kinda creepy, but it's also cool to be admired for the good I do. He is a loner kid who seems to be kinda lost in the world. His father left his mother when he was just three years old, leaving his mother to raise him on her own. So from time to time I help Ms. Cruse and take out Madison to be sort of a big brother to him. It's kinda cool because I don't have any siblings. We're both missing father figures in our lives, so I try to be there for him as much as I can.

"Hey, Madison. What's going on?"

"Nothing much." His hands are still holding up his head. His eyes are fixed on the ground.

"Come on. It's me you're talking to. You can tell me anything."

"I know. It's just that…." He catches himself in his thought and I give him some space to finish. "These kids at school bother me." He lets out a big sigh and continues, "Today was bad, because during reading Ms. Garrett called on me to read aloud… and when I did I kept stuttering all my words. I hate reading and I hate school."

"So do I."

"How can you hate it? You're a hero."

"I was a hero. Now I am just an average kid like you."

"No, you're not. You are the Kid Ranger." Those words sent a ping into my heart.

It still is hard for me to not be donning the tights and cape and flying around the city. It has been three years since I lost my powers. It did not happen overnight, it was something that happened over time. At first I thought it was just some evil genius who put some spell over me, but I learned that I just grew out of them. Those two years of being pricked and prodded by doctors trying to figure out what happened to me was awful. The doctors even sought the help of the Society of Superheroes, but what they figured out is that I was just growing up and losing them.

"I was the Kid Ranger. Now I am just Zak Raven, hero at large." As I say this to Madison, I grab him and toss him over a shoulder and lightly drop him to the ground.

"Evildoers beware!" This makes him laugh out loud. "Hey you wanna see something cool?"

"Sure thing!" he cries out, laughing.

I help him up, grab my backpack and pull out LEO.

"A football?" he questions.

"No, it is a robot. He was given to me by the Superhero Society."

"What does he do?"

"Hmmm… Let's find out." I pull out the manual, set it aside and push a couple of buttons. LEO makes some beeping sounds and starts floating. We both look in amazement as this football thing is floating before our eyes.

"COOL!" Madison cries out.

I press a couple of buttons on the new wrist communicator Brady gave me. LEO stops in mid-air and does a couple of flips.

"Let me try! Let me try!" Madison cries. It is the first time I have seen him excited about anything in a while.

"OK, but let me read this first." Before I can get the "but" out, Madison hits a couple of buttons on my wrist communicator and LEO falls to the ground like a box of rocks. LEO is lying on the ground like we just killed it.

"What do we do?" Madison looks afraid.

A neighbor's evil cat, Puss Puss, springs from the bushes and looks ready to pounce on LEO. "Oh, great. Ms. Jacobs' cat is loose."

"That cat is evil," I tell him. The cat is preparing to jump when a small light on LEO illuminates.

"He's awake!"

"Um…. He is, and by the color of his eye, he is going to attack. Get down, Madison!" I shield Madison from a blast of light that hits Puss Puss.

The cat looks OK, but his hairs are standing up as he runs back into the bushes.

"Serves him right, nasty cat."

"Sorry."

"It's OK, big guy. Let me read a little more about him before we play with him."

"Sounds good to me."

"I have to get in and do some homework. You OK?"

"Yuppers."

I grab LEO, stick him under my arm and head home.

CHAPTER SEVEN

"Nutty, nutty, nutty… That darn kid." The professor slams his fist down on the counter, knocking over a bunch of test tubes. The spilled chemicals burn a hole in the counter and the professor laughs. "That's going to leave a mark."

As he cleans up the mess on the table, a shrieking alarm goes off. He walks to a giant monitor and sees a blue Honda pull up outside. He pushes a couple of buttons and the car drives into his lair. He circles the car, mumbling "Interesting, very interesting."

"This is going to hold back my plans to create the ultimate, unlimited power source. I need a minion to help me. I've tried the personals and chat rooms, and those temp agencies are no good. I will just have to create one."

He looks up at the sound of another alarm going off. "Ah, coffee's ready."

CHAPTER EIGHT

I'm sitting on my bed, looking at LEO. My room is like most fifteen-year-old boys' rooms, except where most boys have trophies from high school sports; I have official keys to cities and letters from two U.S. presidents. Dirty clothes are all over the place, along with a plate of spaghetti from two weeks ago. My twin-size bed has not been made in three months, when my aunt came to visit and my mother forced me to make it.

My favorite possession is a telescope that belonged to my father. From time to time, I take it out to the hills and pretend my father is with me, looking at the stars. The loss of my father has made a big impact on me. I have lots of responsibilities besides saving the day. With my mother working a full-time job, I occasionally have to make dinner and help keep the rest of the house clean. My least favorite chore is mowing the lawn Sunday mornings, because I can't sleep in.

There is a knock on my bedroom door, but the stereo is turned up so loud I don't hear it. The door opens. It's my mother.

"Zak!" she cries out over the music. "Zak!" she yells again, but I'm lying down on the bed with my back to the door and don't hear her.

I'm holding LEO when its eye beam glows and it begins floating again. A beam of light shoots from its eye, over my head and blasts my mom, freezing her in the doorway. I quickly look over my shoulder to see my mom standing there, frozen in time.

"Oh, no," I mumble. I walk to her and wave a hand in front of her eyes. There is no movement. "What did you do to her?" I scream at LEO, who is still floating in the air.

"The intruder is cryonically frozen," LEO says in a cold robotic tone.

"Intruder? That's my mom."

"Mom. That does not compute."

"You know, mother, maternal figure, parent, mommy."

"The matriarch of Zak Raven."

"Yes, now unfreeze her."

"The frozen state is temporary, limited to five minutes, Raven."

She is standing with her mouth open. As I poke her arm, her skin feels cold to the touch. I push on her to see if she will move, but she is one hundred percent frozen, just like a Popsicle.

"This actually could be kinda fun. Now listen here, Sandra Raven, I will not clean up my room, nor will I sweep the gutters. As for the trash, you will take it out. I don't feel like going to school tomorrow. And I get a raise in my allowance. That's right, you heard me, lady." I'm giggling until I see my mother's lips moving.

"Zakery Marvin Raven!" she screams.

"Yikes!" I say under my breath.

"Not only will you clean the gutters, but you will be painting the house this weekend."

"Umm... I'm guessing you heard all that."

"And you will be weed-whacking the side yard. Yes, I heard what you said, young man. What in blazes is that thing?"

"Brady gave him to me. He thinks I need a sidekick."

LEO hovers over to my mother. "He is a cute little thing," she says, "like a football with wings." LEO and

Mom are checking each other out. LEO scans her eyes to register her in its memory banks.

"Don't worry, Mom, it needs to do this to everyone who is close to me. It did it to Madison earlier. I'm guessing it is so it doesn't freeze you again."

"That is a very good idea, Zak. Now dinner is ready, so wash up and come eat."

"What is for dinner?"

"Meatloaf."

"Blech. I think that is worse than some of the villains I have fought."

CHAPTER NINE

Torrance sees her father walk through the back door and ask him in her sweet voice, "Daddy, where have you been all night?"

"Kitten-face, Daddy was working." He takes a piece of bacon from a platter on the counter and notices a new piece of paper on the bulletin board.

"I need you to sign this field trip form to the space museum," Torrance says.

"Ah, yes, the space museum. I used to love going there and seeing all the exhibits. When I was your age, they were sending monkeys into space." He signs his name on the dotted line and hands Torrance the permission slip. Then he pulls out his wallet and gives her twenty dollars. Can you pick me up a shaky globe?"

"No problem, Daddy."

"I'm going to wash up before breakfast."

CHAPTER TEN

"Zak, get up, you are going to be late." My mother opens my bedroom door and LEO is floating at her eye level. She jumps a little but that does not stop him from scanning her eyes.

"Good AM, Mrs. Raven."

"Good AM to you, LEO."

"Did Mrs. Raven have a good slumber?"

"Yes, LEO, I did."

"Five more minutes, Mom" I toss the pillow over my head in order to shut all the light and the mindless chattering going on in my room.

"Raven, the mother figure instructed you to get out of bed." LEO floats down the edge of my bed and flips it over.

"Hey!" I scream as I can hear my mother's laughter in the background. "You are supposed to be on my side!"

"Raven must listen to the matriarch," LEO spouts out.

I get up, shower and have a nutritious breakfast because LEO says it is necessary that I have one. It is worse than my mother and Brady put together. And it is going to be with me at all times. This is going to get old fast.

LEO has turned into another parent. The one thing I miss in the mornings when my father was alive was him calling out to me to have a good day. No matter if he was on a trip, he would always call me in the morning. My father was the greatest and my biggest fan in the superhero days. Part of me feels like I have let him down since I lost my powers. I was like the town all-star. Now I am just a regular kid with a flying robot on his way for a day off of school to attend a field trip.

I turn onto the main drag on my bike and run into Tyler on his skateboard. He grabs onto the back of my bike and LEO shoots a beam at his hands. He cries out in pain and hits the curb and flies into a bush.

"LEO, no!" I yell out. "He is my friend." I skid out on my bike and run to Tyler, who is holding his head and covered in brush. "Are you OK?" As bad as it sounds, it is kinda funny to see him like this.

"What IS that thing?"

"This is the surprise that Brady had for me, my back-up."

"I liked it so much better when you were a solo artist."

LEO scans Tyler's eyes and confirms him into its database.

"LEO, I'm not going to have anyone in my life if you keep doing this."

"Sorry, Tyler. He is learning. Let's go."

We make it safely to school. A bunch of kids are getting on the bus. Mr. Brady is standing outside the bus, checking people in. I lock up my bike and Tyler and I run to the bus. I am jamming LEO into my backpack. "You have to stay in here. I have a hard enough time explaining you to my friends and family."

Tyler and I are out of breath when we get to the bus. "Hey, Mr. Brady."

"Better late than never, Mr. Raven." Brady looks at him with disapproval.

I swear, before I met Brady I had only two parents, now it seems like I have three: mom, Brady and now LEO.

"I got this new alarm clock," I tell Brady. "Instead of hitting the snooze bar in the morning, the snooze bar hits me and flips my bed over."

"I see you and LEO are getting along."

"Yeah, so far it froze my mother and almost killed Tyler. You should have seen what it did to my neighbor's cat."

"Sorry about the scare, Mr. Kruse," Brady says to Tyler.

"No problem, Mr. Brady," Tyler replies.

"We can chitchat about this later; we have a field trip to get underway. Now, will the two of you please get on the bus?"

The bus is crowded with tons of people. I see Torrance sitting with her friends, and what I don't notice is Colton sitting two seats in front of her. I am staring at her when all of a sudden I trip on what I find out is Colton's foot. I hear a bunch of laughs and giggles as I am picking myself up. I can also feel LEO trying to figure out what is going on and trying to get out of the backpack.

"LEO, stop," I whisper to him. This is going to be a long day.

CHAPTER ELEVEN

The lights are low in the laboratory where Professor Raine is working on a project on the examining table. Wearing what looks like a miner's hat and with a tool belt on, he is piecing together a human body made out of metal. There are many robotic body parts on the floor that have been used and reused from previous robots. There are old pizza boxes and smoothie cups all around the laboratory. It looks like he has been down there for days without a break. He grabs his soldering gun and begins welding an arm into place.

"This should get rid of that pesky kid. He fouled up my plans for the last time," he says to himself. "Most important of all, I will not have to do my own filing." Raine's stomach growls and he looks at his watch. "It seems like I missed lunchtime."

Raine goes to the phone and dials a number. "Hello, Leaning Tower of Pizza? I would like to order a pepperoni calzone with extra cheese. Hold on for a second. Would you like one, my friend?" A groan from beneath the sheet on the table confirms his order. "I would like to make that two." Another moan comes from the sheet. "OK, OK, make one with sausage instead of pepperoni, plus one order of buffalo wings and a diet cola." Another groan and Raine adds, "Don't forget about the dipping sauce for the wings." He hangs up the phone and laughs a sinister and uncontrollable laugh. A second laugh comes from the sheet. Each is trying to out-laugh the other.

"Umm, Hello? Hello????" comes a voice from the phone.

"Did you hear something?" Raine wipes the tears of laughter from his eyes.

"Hey! You forgot to hang up the phone!" the voice from the phone screams.

"Sorry, my mistake," Raine says as he puts the receiver back on the phone and resumes his laughter.

CHAPTER TWELVE

We are walking through the museum, listening to the tour guide give his monotone speech on space exploration and the Galileo spacecraft. "Launched in October 1989, Galileo required almost six years to reach Jupiter after looping Venus once and sailing around the Earth twice. The Galileo spacecraft was designed to make a detailed study of Jupiter and its rings and moons over a period of years."

I am walking with Tyler, trying to listen to him and the tour guide at the same time. "We should try it," Tyler tells me. "Everyone at school seems to be into it."

"I know, but who really believes in it? I think it is kinda hokey. And why would I want to be a grape ape anyway?"

"Because Torrance might be a grape ape and you will have something in common. I know that I am an orange lemur."

"These tests are sooo not right. How could it be that you find your mate by answering a bunch of questions about relationships?"

"Zak, don't be a stick in the mud."

"I am not going to conform to what everyone else is doing."

I hear Colton talking to Torrance about the fact that he is a pomegranate lion. She laughs and tells him that she is a peach seal. Mr. Brady hushes us and tells us to listen about the first meal on the moon. Someone blurts out "cheese!" There are a couple of giggles. The tour guide continues, "No, actually it was four bacon squares, three sugar cookies, peaches, coffee and a pineapple-grapefruit drink for Neil Armstrong and Edwin Aldrin Jr. in 1969 before their historical moonwalk."

Colton yells, "Hey, Mark! You are a grapefruit, right?" Going on field trips is not Mr. Brady's favorite thing to do. He tells Colton to hush up.

"Come on, Tyler. This is just a fad that will be replaced soon by some electronic pet."

"Well, it seems you are ahead of the game, because you have one of those, too."

"LEO is not a pet, he is an annoyance. At least he is quiet now."

We file into the planetarium and find some seats. The tour guide speaks up as the lights dim. We're all sitting in chairs with our heads propped upward, which reminds me of my dentist's office. We stare at the ceiling, waiting for the light show to start. Images of the moon and Earth light up on the screen above our heads. The tour guide who we now learn is named Dale is using a laser pointer and says, "Since the moon's orbit is elliptical, its distance varies from about 221,463 miles at the perigee, to 251,968 miles at apogee." He is cut off when someone asks him about what a perigee is. "Good question. It is the point in the orbit of the moon at which it is farthest from the earth."

"So it has nothing to do with dogs?" the kid asks.

"That is a pedigree," Mr. Brady sighs.

"Planets emit a constant light or shine, while stars appear to twinkle. The twinkling effect is caused by a combination of the distance between the stars and the earth and the reactive effect Earth's atmosphere has on a star's light." Someone in the back row is snoring.

"Jameson, wake Wilcox up. This is not naptime," Brady snaps.

The tour guide appears a bit fed up, but he probably deals with this all the time. "Planets are closer to Earth than stars, and their circular shape averages out the twinkling effect." The tour guide uses the laser pointer to outline the constellations, which is really cool. The tour goes on for another thirty minutes before we are let out for lunch.

CHAPTER THIRTEEN

After what seems like days in the planetarium, we are set free to eat our bagged lunches. We are warned by Brady not to venture far from the lawn. Brady can't get enough of this place. He is still talking to the tour guide while the rest of us are eating lunch. It is a beautiful day out. You can see for miles from the viewpoint where we're sitting. It seems like we are high over the city in another peaceful world. I am sitting with Tyler on the grass, watching Colton and Torrance sitting on the fence overlooking the valley below.

"Fine. I will do the test," I tell Tyler to shut him up.

He pulls the romance test out of his bag and hands it to me. I flip through it and notice it has about a hundred questions that range from "What is your favorite pasta?" to "In a dangerous situation, how would you behave?" I don't see the fun in doing this, yet my best friend is going to pester me until I finish with it. I put it in my backpack, making sure not to wake LEO.

"That could be you sitting with Torrance," Tyler mentions to me while pointing to the brick wall where Torrance is sitting. Colton is acting like a monkey for her, jumping up and down and trying to do a back flip with a friend's help.

"Tyler, there are two types of people in this world: people like them and people like us. The two groups never merge."

"You fight crime all the time, but you are afraid to go up to her and talk to her."

"I'm not afraid. I'm just… Umm… OK, fine. I'm afraid."

A bunch of kids are playing football. The ball flies over to where we are sitting on the grass. I pick it up and throw it back. Fortunately, my uncle taught me how to throw a football. "Wow, I am shocked, not even a 'thank you.'"

I look over to where Torrance is sitting on the wall and see Colton holding her feet while she is leaning over the edge.

Tyler sees what I am looking at and says, "Now that's a bright idea."

Torrance looks scared, and I can see her telling Colton "Please stop, Colton! Leave my feet alone. Come on. Stop, Colton!" Then, in a flash, I watch the football sail into Colton's head. He grabs his head with both hands, letting go of Torrance's feet. She screams as she flips over the ledge.

"Hey! Watch where you throw that!" Colton yells. "Oh, my god! TORRANCE! Somebody help her! Mr. Brady!"

Brady is on the other side of the lawn, still chatting away with the tour guide. His back it turned to the wall and he doesn't see Torrance fall.

I jump to my feet and run to the wall. Torrance is clinging to a sewage pipe twenty feet below. The pipe is the only thing keeping her from plummeting two hundred feet. It is covered in sewage, making it difficult to grasp, and spewing tainted water on Torrance and the rocks below. A crowd gathers to see the spectacle. From the edge, I roll up my sleeve to reveal my communicator. I tap a couple of buttons and a thin grappling hook comes out of it. Another button and the grappling hook shoots down to the pipe.

"Grab the line!" I scream down to her.

"I'm scared! I can't let go!" Her fingers are turning blue from holding tightly to the pipe.

"You have to trust me!"

"I can't!" she screams.

Brady sees the commotion and heads for the crowd.

Colton pushes his way to the front of the onlookers. He grabs me to push me out of the way. I stand my ground with him for the first time in my life. "Don't be a moron," I tell him, "I am not going to save two people, and if I have to pick one, it's not going to be you." He's stunned that I just mouthed off to him. "Fine, freakboy…. Just do something."

"I'm slipping!" Torrance yells, and one of her hands slips off the pole.

Brady runs in to do crowd control. Brady does not have all the faith in me when it comes to homework, but when it comes to saving people, his faith shows. "Everyone, move away and give them some space," Brady tells the kids, but no one moves. "I said now, unless you want detention." That seemed to do it. Threaten them with after-school activities that include counting the hairs on your arm.

"Grab the rope, I'll pull you up!" I yell down to Torrance. She reaches for it with her free hand for a moment before grabbing the pipe again, only this time she clutches a patch of soggy moss. She loses her grip and falls toward the rocks below. The crowd screams with Torrance as she falls. Using nothing but instinct, I jump off the wall, holding the base of my grappling hook. The other end of the hook is wrapped around the pole. It has been a while since I have felt a freefall. I straighten my body like an arrow going down after Torrance. The wind is blowing hard, and all I hear is silence, even though there is screaming above. I pass Torrance while hitting a couple of buttons on my communicator. The wire from the grappling hook tightens. In one fluid motion, I swing below her and grab her around her waist.

"Hold on!" I scream.

"OK!"

A brush of her hair glides across my arm. Her tears are spraying me, too. As we swing, I know this is going to be a difficult landing.

"You need to brace yourself for the impact," I tell her.

"What are you talking about?" Her eyes light up as she grabs me forcefully.

We swing into the mountainside and get the wind knocked out of us. My body shields hers from most of the impact, and I feel like I've crushed several ribs. Now really dizzy, I push the up button on my communicator. The grappling hook wire retracts, lifting Torrance and me back to the pipe. Fire trucks arrive and lower a rope ladder to us. Sirens are blaring in the background. Torrance is still in shock; I can feel her shivering in my arms. All I can think about is the smell of her hair in my face.

After what seems like years, a couple of firefighters pull us up to and over the railing. There is a big scene around us now. Paramedics race to us with their gear and check us for injuries. Brady is trying to regain control of the crowd, with little luck. He's holding my backpack to make sure LEO doesn't make a debut. LEO is supposed to be a secret weapon — which means the general public is not to see it. Someone is asking me a bunch of questions that just sound like noise. My head is throbbing and I black out.

CHAPTER FOURTEEN

I remember when I learned I had superpowers. I was about three years old and playing in the sandbox with my cousins. Scott, who is my age, had a toy I really wanted to play with, but he wouldn't share. I cried and pounded my fists into the sand. My eyes glowed a reddish glow. I could feel the rage growing inside me as a beam of light shot out of my eyes, hitting the toy in his hand. He screamed, which made me scream even more. Our mothers ran over to us. Scott's mom grabbed him, taking him to sit on the bench with her. My mother saw the red glow in my eyes and watched it fade. She was frightened a bit but picked me up and sang to me. Her voice always put me at ease. For the next couple of years, I attended meetings with my parents to help me learn to control my powers. Those meetings are where I made the connections that would eventually make me a junior member of the Superhero Society.

I sense a light in my eyes as I open them. All I can muster out of my mouth is a little moan of pain. I squint into the light and see an angel looking over me. "Am I dead?" I ask. The angel laughs, "No, silly, you are in the hospital."

"Torrance?"

"Yes, I wanted to make sure you were OK." She turns away from me. "I am really sorry that you had to save me because Colton was being a twit."

"Hey it's all in day's work." I sit up and feel a shooting pain in my ribs. "Owwww!" I yell, clutching my sides. As I yell, my mother and Tyler walk into the room. "What happened? Why am I in here? Did I miss the rest of the tour?" I ask. "I wanted to see the giant telescope."

"You blacked out," my mother tells me. There's sadness in her voice. She is frightened that something will happen to me. I'd told her I would be really careful. It's not fair for her to lose another loved one.

"You're my hero," Tyler laughs. It seems to break the tension in the room.

"Gee, thanks." I lie back down.

"They are just bruised and not broken, you were lucky," my mother says. "This does not mean you will get out of school. You will be released tomorrow."

A nurse pops her head in the doorway and announces, "You have another visitor, Mr. Raven." My mother walks to the door, saying, "Thank you so much for coming, Mr. Raine. I'm sure that Zak would love to talk to you."

"Wonderful. I knew his father well back in the days of college."

"That's odd, he never mentioned it," my mother says curiously.

"We had a falling out over a lovely girl. We all were in a class together; I sat three rows in back of you, Mrs. Raven."

"I never noticed. You should have said something."

"That's not my style, then a couple of months later I met Torrance's mother."

"Would you mind if I had a moment alone with the esquire Raven? Torrance, would you please wait for me in the waiting room?"

"Sure, Dad."

The crew of people who came to visit me leaves Raine and me alone.

"Zak. May I call you Zak?" he asks.

"Umm… sure."

"Thank you for saving my little girl. She is all I have since her mother died. I do not know what I would do without her. You are a little hero, my hero." His tone gets a little weird. "You are going to have to come over to our house for a smoothie."

"Umm… OK." Then it hits me: I am invited to Torrance's house, even if it is for a mixed-fruit beverage.

"So, may I ask you a question?" Raine asks, sitting on the end of the bed.

"Sure thing, Mr. Raine."

"Where do you get all those lovely toys?"

"What are you talking about?"

"The grabbling hook, the explosives and this…" He pulls out LEO from behind his back.

OK, this is getting weird. Why did this man go through my backpack?

"That is my new… electronic football game." He turns LEO over and over in his hands, analyzing it. All I can think of is that LEO is going to turn on and zap Mr. Raine with some sort of ray. When he shakes LEO, I hold my breath but nothing happens. I guess Brady shut him down during the commotion.

My mother walks in. She caresses my head the same way she did when I was really young. "You should get some rest now, honey."

"Rest, yes the esquire should rest, he had a busy day," Raine says. He turns around at the door. "I will see you again soon, Zak."

"Oh, yes, the smoothie thing. Definitely."

"Yes, the smoothie." He walks out the door.

I am thinking to myself how odd that conversation was when a nurse comes in and gives me something to help me sleep. I drift off again.

CHAPTER FIFTEEN

It was great staying home from school for a couple of days. I got to catch up on my talk shows, infomercials and soap operas. Not that I am a big fan of any of those, I just liked being a vegetable on the couch. My mother would come home for lunch to make sure I was fed. I could get used to this life. The only thing that stinks is that my mother asked Tyler to bring me my homework. When he comes over, we talk about what is going on at school and play "Space Neutron." A couple of bumps and bruises will not get in my way of playing my video games. At least it is a light load of homework while I am away. I have to finish a paper for my U.S. History class on one of the presidents. I usually wait until the last minute to do my homework, which I know is not the most responsible thing. I still haven't picked the president I want to do it on, there are so many to choose from.

After my rest and relaxation, I am back at school. I have a couple of bruised ribs that are bandaged pretty tightly and hidden under my clothes. The bad news is that everything is back to normal. I am still ignored by everyone; the only difference is that Colton's insults have stopped for now. He just pretends I am not even around. I'm sure this will change in time. The bell rings while I am walking down the hall to Ms. Eisen's English class. Thanks to Tyler, I finished my reading my assigned chapters in Shakespeare's "Romeo and Juliet." It is not the easiest thing I've read, with all the "thous" and other odd Old English terms. Thank goodness for crib notes to help me decipher what the story is about.

"Zak!" I hear my name being called from down the hall. I'm sure they're calling someone else, like Jack or Mac. The voice screams out the name again. Maybe it's Tack. Why would anyone be calling out Tack? I give into temptation and am surprised when I turn around and see it's Torrance.

"Hey," I tell her.

"I'm glad that you're back. Are you feeling better?"

"Thanks, the swelling has gone down a lot."

There is a lull in the conversation, and the only thing that pops out of my mouth is, "What is your favorite type of Jell-O?" I almost die of embarrassment from the lame question I just asked her.

"That's a new one."

"Sorry, I meant to ask how you are feeling."

"Fine, and grape," she says.

"Mine is lime." The lull is back, only this time I cannot come up with a thing to say to her.

"Speaking of fruits, this fell out of your pocket during all the craziness at the observatory. I meant to give it to you at the hospital." She hands me the fruit romance test. "Have you taken it yet? I am a peach seal."

"No, not yet," I tell her. "Knowing me, I am going to be a tomato, though I'm not totally convinced that it is a real fruit."

I get a smile from her. "It's pretty corny."

We have not had a normal conversation since she asked me to get off the see-saw in the second grade. The bell rings, she says she has to go to class and that she will see me around. Maybe my luck is changing.

CHAPTER SIXTEEN

Because I am still bruised, my mother picks me up from school. We have the normal homework chitchat.

"Are you going to the big football game tonight?" she asks.

"Yeah, Tyler and I are going to go there for a bit."

"Are you going to see Torrance?"

"Dunno."

"She is a very nice girl; I liked her father, too. I am a bit surprised that I don't remember him from college." She goes on about the college days until we pull into the driveway. Madison is sitting at the front door. My mother lets me out and drives back to work.

"Hey, big guy, what's going on?"

"Nothing, I wanted to see if you were all right."

"I'm fine, just a couple of scratches."

"Was it an evil villain who did this to you?" His eyes light up, wanting to hear an exciting story.

I promised never to lie to the kid. "Nah, just a dumb high school jock."

Madison's mother is calling him in to finish his homework. We say our goodbyes and I tell him if he needs any help with the homework to come on by.

I toss my backpack on the floor, dreading the fact that I have to go back to school for this lame football game. Sometimes I wonder how Tyler talks me into these things. I know I am supposed to have school sprit, but after the day I had, all I want to do is veg out in front of my video game console. Until then, I have a few hours to kill, so I pull it out and play "Space Neutron." This is the one game where I can take out my aggression on the bad guys.

In all my years, I have been to space only once. It was on a mission with the Yellow Krill. When you think about it, I should have been traveling the seven seas with the Krill instead of space. I am one of a few people who gets to call him by his first name, Jason.

Jason was born inside the stomach of a whale. His mother was from Atlantis and was swallowed whole by a blue whale while out swimming. Inside the whale's stomach his mother ate nothing but krill, which gave him his superpower — the ability to shoot glowing rays in complete darkness. Jason's mother spent months inside the whale before giving birth. Soon after Jason was born, a whaling ship trapped the blue whale. Noticing the water level was getting dangerously low, Jason's mother yelled for help. A fisherman heard the cries, sliced open the whale and found both mother and child. Her dying wish was that the fisherman takes care of her son, which he did.

Jason was raised in regular public school. He knew he was different from the other kids because at night he would glow. As he got older, he was able to control the glowing and use it to fight evil. This is when I met him. We were both members of the Secret Society of Superheroes. We were sent on a mission to space to test the new space cruiser. It is so embarrassing to have to get a permission slip signed by your mother to go to space. On the mission we had to measure the circumference of the earth. This needs to be done every two years to make sure the planet is the same size. Even a fraction of growth can alter humanity. Not only did we learn the planet from pole to pole is 24,860 miles, but we measured the distance around the earth at the equator, 24,902 miles. I got to see a lot of cool a unique things like a meteor shower and the craters of the moon.

We took a detour to the moon to see it up close. While I was watching the moon from the cockpit, I heard a thump. I looked at Jason, who put his finger over his mouth to hush me up. All the lights went off in the craft. I am used to danger, but not this far from home. All of a sudden, the door to the cockpit blasted inward. Two space pirates appeared. One flashed his light into my eyes. "It's just a kid," he growled.

"Um, the parrot gotta go," I told him. I stalled while Jason maneuvered himself into position to take them both down. I knew the drill from chapter fifteen of the Secret Society Handbook.

"A little snot-nosed brat," he chimed off. "We want the space satellite, then we will be off." They hit the wrong spacecraft and the chatty pirate's third-grade education was wearing me down.

"Hey, guy, this is the Secret Society of Superheroes' spacecraft and not the Soviet Sputnik Space Station." After telling him this, I heard a gulp. The flashlight was looking all around for other people in the ship. They didn't see Jason yet.

He turned to the other pirate and said, "The kid is alone."

"Actually, I am. And I was wondering if you could help me get back to Earth, I'm scared." I whined and sniffled like I was going to cry.

He shined the light on some rope on the floor. "Mick, get the kid and tie him up. I'll check the controls."

I could take these guys in a second, I thought, but being a junior member not in full control of my powers meant I had to wait because I could knock them into something or hurt them. I heard Jason make a peep. He actually used the word "peep," and I laughed before shutting my eyes, knowing peep was his code word. Jason shot a giant blast of energy into the room and froze everyone who had their eyes open.

An hour later, after the effects wore off, the two pirates were tied together on the floor and moaning. I never figured out which hurt them more: the blast of energy or the camp songs Jason and I sang on our way back to Earth.

You have a lot of time to get to know someone on a trip like that. Jason and I remain pen pals. He tells me all about his adventures. Sometimes I wish I still had powers so I could pal around the globe with him again.

After a couple hours in front of the tube, playing my game, I hear my mother come home and yell for me to clean up my room before I leave. I know that I will get in trouble for this, but I pull LEO out of its container and tell it to clean the room. Life is good with a robot maid. I now can say I have something in common with the Jetsons. After a good hour of folding, dusting and organizing my CD collection, LEO rests in front of me, watching the computer game. I can't get past the level where the Space Lord takes the Pulsar Star. LEO keeps staring at it and says, "Enter four, two, sixty six, eight onto screen." I am stunned that it's speaking to me after all this time. It says it again.

"OK, OK," I tell it and type the numbers into the screen. There is a flash on the screen. The Space Lord has blown up.

"How did you know about this?" I turn to LEO in surprise. It does not speak but looks intrigued by what I am playing.

"Do you want to try it?" I ask.

"Affirmative." Mechanical hands extend from LEO's little football body and it hovers over the floor, blasting bad guys. I am so awed by what LEO is doing that I don't notice the time. Tyler walks into my room and his jaw drops.

"What a trip," I tell him.

"I know what I want for Christmas," he laughs.

It's time to leave. I try taking the joystick from LEO, but it's no good. It will not let go, and its eye is fixed on the screen.

"What do I do?" I sound panicked. "What if I broke it? Brady is going to kill me. I got this million-dollar robot hooked on video games! What if it never lets go?"

"Pull the plug," Tyler says.

I reach for the plug, and LEO's eye turns toward me and shoots a red beam at my hands. "Ouch! Now what?"

"I dunno, but if we don't leave now, we are going to miss the kickoff."

I can either do the responsible thing and try to figure this out, or I can go to the football game, see Torrance and then come home and figure it out.

"Grab my jacket, over there." I shut my bedroom door on the way out and yell to my mother that we're leaving for the game.

CHAPTER SEVENTEEN

Football games in Bluffside are a big deal. People arrive at the stadium at least an hour before the game for tailgate parties. Everyone shows off their school spirit by wearing our school colors of orange and blue. The Cougars logo is plastered all over town on posters and banners. It is kinda strange how the town supports a high school team more than the national football league or even the local college.

The kickoff begins with a bang. The visiting team is on the defensive, or it is the offensive? Let's just say the ball is in the air and the other team is going to catch it and run with it down the field. I will never win sportsman of the year.

I scan the bleachers for Torrance or anyone I know. She is sitting near the top, decked out in her best orange and blue and has the worst looking accessory around her: Colton.

"You would think that dumping you off a wall into a cavern of doom would constitute a breakup," I tell Tyler over the roars of cheers.

"You would think," he laughs.

The game goes on forever. Ryan Wright is the worst punter in the Cougars' history. His average yards per kick has set record lows in the state. His father is a bigwig in Bluffside. Giving lots of money to the football booster club ensures that his son stays on the team. It's always fun to watch Ryan miss the ball and fall. It makes the admission price worth every penny.

There are some giggles in the crowd as Ryan runs up to the ball, punting it over the full length of the football field. The crowd that was giggling is in stunned silence. Nobody knows what to think, including the opposing team. A player for the Warriors grabs the ball and runs with it. The Cougars charge for him. Ryan speeds up, passing his teammates and steamrolling down the field toward the gathering Warriors. The Warriors form a human wall to block Ryan from passing, yet Ryan bowls right into them, sending bodies flying into the air.

"Zak, are you seeing this?" Tyler says.

Ryan is running straight for the Warrior with the ball.

"I see it, but I don't believe it." I grab the binoculars from the guy next to me to look at Ryan. At the top of his helmet I see a radio transmitter. His eyes are glowing red.

"That's not Ryan, that thing is not even human!"

I jump down onto the field, pushing a couple of buttons on my communicator. I shoot my grappling hook over the goal post. Luckily I am a good shot, grabbing the Warrior guy's jersey. I yank really hard, and the football player is lifted into the air as Ryan arrives to mow him down.

Everyone's watching Ryan and not noticing what I am doing. Ryan runs under the Warrior and slams into the goal post so hard it falls down. People in the stands are screaming. I run through the crowd after Ryan, who left the stadium and is in the parking lot. I am a bit winded when I reach him. He is standing still like a statue.

"Ryan, you OK?" He turns around for me to see his glowing eyes.

In a robotic tone comes one word, "Zak."

This is gonna be bad. I feel a thump as I'm thrown back by his punch to the chest. I land on a parked car, cracking the window. "You better have a low deductible," I say out loud. Feeling the pain, I get up and leap in

Ryan's direction. He is literally taking off. He has some sort of foot rockets in his shoes that lift him into the sky. I am going to have to talk to Brady about getting some of those. I still have the binoculars around my neck when I look up to see a huge blimp floating a hundred feet above me. The Ryan robot gets into the blimp and takes off in a flash.

Tyler runs over to me, telling me that they found the real Ryan tied up in the locker room. He was hit from behind and didn't see who hit him.

"The robot was meant to scare me off," I tell Tyler.

"Are you sure your ego is not getting to you?"

"He called me by name."

The rest of the game is cancelled. I get out of there before anyone can ask me questions. Last thing I want to do today is have to deal with the Bluffside PD.

At home, I walk into my room to find LEO still playing the video game.

"Great, my sidekick is a video game junkie."

CHAPTER EIGHTEEN

The doors open to the cabin of the cockpit of the blimp. The robot version of Ryan steps through.

"Just as planned, you did well," Professor Raine laughs. "Causing havoc in this little town just to get Zak Raven expelled is so worth the risks. Once expelled, the boy will have to leave Bluffside, then I will take over the town, then the world." He paces the floor of the cockpit. "Where was that football robot of his? I was sure that it was going to make an appearance. I need to know where he gets his toys."

The robot Ryan sheds his football uniform, putting on a green and blue costume that Raine has given him. Raine laughs along with the robot Ryan at his side. They are trying to outdo their evil laughs.

Raine has a sour look on his face, noticing that his robot is out-evil-laughing him. He picks up the robot and flips off its power. The robot's eyes go blank and the laughing stops. Professor Raine feels good about himself that he won the contest. The blimp sails off into the distance.

CHAPTER NINETEEN

Ciara Monet is in my third-period history class. I did not get my homework done, so I asked her if I could copy her homework really fast. I know this is bad, but I need the extra points.

Ciara is one of the smartest people in my grade. He parents have high hopes for her, since her older sister never went to college and is working at the Taco Kingdom full time. Ciara is destined to attend an Ivy League school and probably will become a doctor or a lawyer. I have known her as long as Torrance. Ciara is aware that I've had a crush on her since the second grade, but she keeps it to herself because I know that she has liked Tyler for same amount of time. During the days when I had superpowers, Ciara would always come to my rescue when school stuff was involved. She would drop off homework on her way home. There were even the nights when she came for dinner to tutor me. Our parents are good friends, which sometimes puts pressure on her social calendar. She is popular while I am very much not.

"Zak, you are going to have to do your homework one of these days."

"I know, I was at the football game chasing that Ryan robot thing around."

"I heard you got your butt kicked."

"Wow, news travels fast." I say as Ryan walks past us and into the classroom.

"At least he is OK. I heard the police questioned everyone at the game to see if they knew anything that happened."

"So I am guessing you did not go to the game."

"I'm the one with the completed homework, Einstein."

"Come on, Ciara. Please, can I just see it for a second? I will get you to the Paradise Dance with Tyler." I whine to her, trying to do the puppy dog thing with my eyes.

"Fine, this is the last time I will do this for you. You owe me." She pauses. "But you can't tell him I like him, got it?"

"You have my word," I tell her.

"You do, and I will be worse threat to you than any of the supervillains you have had."

"Even the Human Giblet?"

"Yes, Zak even worse than him… or was that a her?"

"The government is still trying to figure that out."

I grab her paper and start copying it in the hallway before class starts. Neatness does not count at this point. I am writing as fast as I can, trying just to get as much as I can on the paper. It is a bunch of questions about the Civil War. My hand hurts from writing so fast. I am sure that I have spelled Abraham Lincoln wrong. The bell rings and I can feel Ciara's eyes on me, telling me to hurry up. She is not the type to ever be late for class. She grabs the paper and heads in class. I got about ninety percent of the homework copied. At least I know that the answers I copied are going to be correct.

CHAPTER TWENTY

Physical Education class can be the worst. We have this odd teacher who I think has never taken a shower. Her name is Ms. Megan, and she is a quite large gal, who for some reason always eats Oreo's while we are running around the track. Today is the second quarter of the class, when we need to pick teams for softball. We have to break out into four teams. The sucky thing is that I am one of the team captains. Being one of the most unpopular kids in the class does not make it a major fun thing to be picking people. When I pick them, most people roll their eyes and huff. I think this is a tie for being the most uncomfortable, being tied to being picked last out of the class. This happened last quarter for tennis. I was stuck with Ms. Megan as my partner. She has one lazy eye that prevents her from seeing balls that are hit to her backhand. We lost the tournament — actually, we really lost the tournament — and came in last. I have a feeling that this is the reason Ms. Megan made me a captain of one of the softball teams, to make up for the tennis fiasco.

We are in the middle of playing our first game, and I have been playing pretty well, except for the spin I did when I was up to bat. I foul-tipped two balls, which meant I had two strikes. At least I touched the baseball when it was thrown to me. I am concentrating really hard. The ball is pitched and I swing really hard. Not only do I miss the ball completely, but I do a couple of spins around in a circle because of the g-force. I hear giggles. Ms. Megan checks to see if I am OK, which makes it worse. She puts her arm around me and walks me off the plate.

"Can anyone tell me what Zak did wrong?" she yells into the field.

"He was born," someone replies.

Someone on my team answers, "He got the third out?"

Another person calls out, "He's a mama's boy."

The insults keep on coming, and they all blend into one word, "whatamoroncan'thitneedstogoplaycrabball." I've learned to block out their comments.

"Zak, you should choke up on the bat and stop closing your eyes when you swing," she tells me. "At least you did not throw the bat this time. Badminton is next quarter, you might be better at that."

"Thanks for the advice." I walk away humiliated and want to go home.

"Schultz, get your team in and get up to bat," she yells.

The giggles turn into laughs. I grab my baseball glove and slump into the filed. At least I am better at playing out there. I am playing second base when a ball is hit directly to me. I close my eyes and pray that I will catch the ball and then slam, right into my glove. I caught it. My team cheers for me, at least I think it was for me. Seems like things might be changing for me. There is a buzzing sound in the air. It is really loud and sounds like a cappuccino maker blowing up. Everyone stops what they are doing and looks up. The sky above is turning black. The sun is being blocked out. The cloud of darkness is coming closer to the softball field. Ms. Megan is stunned and screams at everyone to get inside. I am still looking up while the other kids throw their gloves and balls down and run into the gym. Kids knock into me on their way past me, but I'm not fazed. I keep looking into the sky as the blackness covers the sky over my head. From what I can tell, they are bugs, a whole lot of bugs.

I take the ball still in my hand and throw it up in the air really hard, up into the blackness of the bugs. The ball disappears into the dark and I smell a weird odor. A minute later, the ball falls back to the earth with a couple of the bugs. I pick up the bugs. I am alone on the field. Everyone, including Ms. Megan, has run for cover.

I examine the bugs and notice they are locusts. Some of them are smashed from the ball I tossed in the air, while others are still intact. I hold one up and it melts in my hand.

"Nasty..." I scream out. The odor smells familiar and worse than Body Odor Brian does, sort of like the stinky cheese my mother loves.

Pepper-jack cheese locusts. This is getting weird. There is a change in the air. It is like the flying cheese locusts are making their way back to me. I think it is because I mashed a couple of their friends.

This is bad. I run off the field toward the school and sense the cheese locusts gathering above me. They are on my tail when I get to the outside lunch area. I hurdle over the blue lunch tables. I get to the last one, flip it on its side and dive behind it. Cheese locusts slam into the table and explode into a stinky mess. Those that don't splatter buzz over my head. More and more locusts pelt the table with such force that the table pushes back. I try to hold up the table, but the force of cheese locusts is too strong for me, and I'm being pushed toward the wall. The locusts want to crush me against the wall. I am pressed to the wall and the pounding of the locusts is getting harder and harder.

"LEO, come in!" I yell into my wrist communicator. It probably went home to play more video games.

Oh, no. I remember that LEO is in my gym locker and the transmission is blocked by the metal walls. I am going to have to talk to Brady about this unless I become a human nacho. Then I catch a glimpse of a heating duct that runs all around the school.

I have one shot at this. I push a couple of buttons on my wrist communicator and shoot my grappling hook into the duct. I tug on the wire, but I don't have enough leverage to pull myself into the duct. Yech, I need to stand up and get pelted by cheese locusts. A spray of cheese hits me in the face as I stand. I will never eat Cheese Whiz again. I yank with all my might and rip the duct down from the top of the school building. I drop back behind the table. A blast of hot air hits the area around me and, one by one, locusts melt and fall to the ground.

I peek over the lunch table and see a mile-long big blob of cheese. I climb over the table and try to step in the few spots on the ground that missed the cheese assault. I'm watching my steps when I run right into Principal Montal. He has a couple of blobs of cheese on his shoulders, and his shoes are covered in gooey globs.

"Do you have anything to say about this mess?" Principal Montal growls at me. "I know you had something to do with this."

"This is not my fault this time, there were these locusts made out of cheese…" I notice a big blob of cheese hanging over his head. "Umm, maybe we should talk in your office."

"We will not. Who is going to clean this up?" He scolded again, "Mr. Raven, how many times have I had to warn you about bringing your superhero antics to school?"

The blob over Montal's head is bulging under its own weight and sagging.

"I had nothing to do with it. It's not my fault this time."

"Mr. Montal, can I speak to you?" Ms. Megan calls from across the hall.

"This is not over, Mr. Raven." His eyes are grilling me.

Part of me wants to warn him about the big cheese blob above his head, and another part hopes it plops right on top of him. I go for the right thing and start to open my mouth.

"Mr. Montal, you should really…" Too late, the cheese blob plops onto Montal's head, covering him in cheese. I back away as a panicked Ms. Megan reaches him, chastising him for running such a dangerous school.

CHAPTER TWENTY ONE

It is 8:15 in the morning and I can hear the bell ringing in the distance. Once again, I am late to school. I pull up to the bike rack and look for a space to lock my bike up, but no space is to be found. I grit my teeth, and all I can think about is getting another tardy. I'll have to go to the office, and chances are I would run into Mr. Montal. I can't handle what he would have to say to me after yesterday's fiasco.

I see a bike space. I clamp my bike down and run off to class, praying that Mr. Esien is in a good mood today.

I sneak into English class but no one is there. I look into the classroom next door and, once again, nobody in there. I see a senior walking in the hall.

"Where is everyone?" I ask.

"There is an assembly in the gym, some sort of career day," he tells me.

I forgot about that. As I rush off to the gym, I pass the lunch tables and notice the cheese has been washed away but it still stinks of cheese. I sneak into the gym. Tables line the room, and there are posters on the walls of people in different occupations. The people behind the tables hand out pamphlets, buttons and candy to students to get them excited about working for the local Coffee Nook of the Fire Department. Of course, the police are here, too. I see Officer Dent talking to a bunch of kids and I decide to walk a different way.

"Mr. Raven." I here my name being called as I walk in front of the Dianetics table.

My stomach drops and all I can think about is how I wish I could change my name. Mr. Raine is sitting behind the table.

"Oh, hey, Mr. Raine. I thought you were the principal."

"Sorry to disappoint you," he laughs.

"Actually, I'm glad it is you and not him."

"So, what are you planning to do with your life?"

"That is a loaded question; I haven't figured it out yet."

A bunch of pamphlets for his company are stacked on the table. "I have always been fond of science," I say and flip through a pamphlet to see what type of programs they have to offer.

"We could use someone like you in our detail," he snickers. "We have internships all the time."

"You have to be a junior to take an internship," I tell him.

"I could talk to the principal and see if I can have that rule waved." He adds, "You did save my daughter's life."

"Thanks anyway, Mr. Raine, I have a lot on my plate right now."

"That's right. How stupid could I be? What with you saving the world and all. So, where do you get all your gadgets? Maybe I can be some help to you."

"Thanks anyway, I got it covered; I have to get moving along." I walk away.

"Mr. Raven," Raine says and I turn around. He is holding something up to hand me. "Would you like a mini cheese wheel?"

Thinking about cheese is the last thing I want to do, but to be nice I walk back and take one from him.

"See ya' later, Mr. Raine." I tell him and walk off to find Tyler or anyone. Ciara is talking to the dentist when I walk up behind her. She takes her free toothbrush and turns to me.

"Don't say a word," she scowls at me.

"Dentist… Impressive."

"Do you always have to be a jerk?" We walk over to the water fountain for a drink.

"Pretty much."

She wipes her mouth. "On that note, I'm outta here."

"Geez, Ciara, why are you so touchy today?" I lean against the wall. "I spoke to Tyler last night, and he is cool about going to the dance"

"And?" She's warming up.

"We will pick you up at seven." I tell her.

"You didn't tell him I liked him, did you?"

"Nope, I just told him that we were going in a big group. Me, you and him."

"That's a really big group, Zak," she tells me in a sarcastic tone.

"Hey, it's not like I am the most popular person to be around. Between you, him and my ten-year-old neighbor, that's my posse. Since Madison has a bedtime of 8 p.m., it looks like it is just the three of us. Unless you want to invite Torrance to go with us."

"Is that all you think about, Torrance?"

"That and saving the town from cheese bugs."

"I heard about that. Rumor says that you had something to do with it."

"Not really, they came out of nowhere during P.E. and I had to do something."

"I was in the office today and heard a meeting going on about you breaking the heating duct. Montal wanted to suspend you but Mr. Brady and Ms. Meagan stood up for you."

"He gives me a headache."

"Did you hear what is for lunch today?"

"Don't tell me…. cheeseburgers," I groan.

"Nope, cheese enchiladas, cheese nachos, fried cheese sticks."

"Isn't there some law that says we have to have some sort of veggie?"

"Oh, did I not mention the broccoli?"

"Let me guess, with a cheese sauce."

"They had to do something with the cheese."

"Umm, throw it away, trash it."

"Mr. Brady did some tests on it and he said it was good."

"Yeah, but he did not have cheese coming out of his ears. I mean it was really coming out of my ears."

"Great visual, Zak."

"I should go find Brady and get some answers but Principal Montal is standing at the door. Could you…?"

"Yes, I will do the espionage thing for you." She approaches Montal and they talk. I can always count on Ciara, the best butt kisser in the ninth grade. They walk away from the door and I make a break for it. I run down the hallway to Brady's classroom.

He is sitting at his desk, looking through a microscope at something. He does not even look up when I enter the room. "I checked all the satellite photos, and the cheese swarm came from Bluffside." He tells me, still looking down.

"I thought we were only famous for the big ball of twine at Mills Ranch, not cheese critters."

"The cheese had to be imported from somewhere. I was up all last night checking into all the cheese distributor accounts and nothing. Tons of cheese does not just show up."

"You gave the OK to serve it to the school?" I ask, sounding confused.

"It was either that or you get suspended."

"Yum-yum, cheese is my friend."

"I thought you would see it that way."

"No biggie, I brought a lunch today. What about the deal with them flying around in bug form after me?"

"I checked the databases, and none of your villains are out and about, except for the Thermostat. I want you to check on it after school."

"The creepy guy that controls the weather. Do you really think that cheese is his M.O.?"

"I'm not going to take any chances, someone is after you and he is from Wisconsin. So we are not taking any chances."

"Going for the long shot."

"Here is his address." He hands me a piece of paper with the address, which is on the outskirts of town.

CHAPTER TWENTY TWO

It was a day that did not seem to end. I hop on my bike and decide that I have the need for speed. I push the button on the controls changing the bike into the motorcycle. I'm off to find the Thermostat's last known address, which is on the outskirts of town. The name Julian Frank is on the mailbox. I get off the motorcycle and walk up the dirt road. I knock on the door and there is no answer. I look through the window for signs of life. I see a couple of cats in the house, so I know that someone lives there. I jump down from the porch and see someone out in the field.

"Excuse me; I'm looking for Julian Frank." I say out loud, walking toward what appears to be a ragged-looking man. No response. "Is he around?" Still no answer. I get to the man and realize I'm talking to a scarecrow.

"I'm glad nobody was here to see this," I tell myself.

"You're trespassing on private property!" a voice yells at me. I spin around to see a man pointing a rifle at me. The man is really old and feeble and I don't recognize him. With one jump I could take him down in the blink of the eye. No need for violence, yet.

"Hold on, I'm looking for Julian Frank. Does he still live here?"

"Who wants to know?" he says, still holding the gun.

"You can put the gun down, guy. I mean you no harm." That did not seem to work, I hear the click of the hammer. He is not going to put it down.

"I asked you a question," he says.

"My name is Zak Raven, I knew Julian."

"Zak Raven, hmmm. Wait, you're that snot-nosed brat, the Kid Ranger. You had my son put away!" The gun is still fixed on me, and I am getting uncomfortable. In the distance I see something flying this way at superspeed. I try to keep calm. He rambles about how I put his son in jail. The flying thing gets close enough for me to recognize that it's LEO. It is directly behind the man, and my eyes widen.

"Oh, no," I mumble under my breath.

He spins around and sees LEO.

"Oh, my! What is that contraption?" He pulls the trigger and LEO moves a little to the right to dodge the bullet. I run and jump to tackle the old man and LEO shoots out a net that gets me instead of the old man.

"This is not good," I say.

I am sitting on the ground with a net over me. The old man gets up and grabs his gun. I push a couple of buttons on my wrist communicator and tell LEO to stall. LEO falls out of the sky.

"What is going on here? Start talking before I start shootin'." I can tell he is really upset.

"Your son, I need to know where he is. There was a crime committed and I want to make sure he is clear of it."

"My son has given up crime and is following his passion."

"Father, what is going on here?" Through the net I see a middle-aged man in overalls walking over to me. "Hello, Zak."

"Julian, I told him that you are innocent, that you are no longer doing crime," the man tells his son.

"I know, Father. Can you please leave us alone?" Julian says. "Take the gun with you, I can handle the situation."

"OK, boy, if you need me you just holler." The old man walks to the house.

"Hey, Thermostat, how are the wife and kids?"

"I see you are going for the net look, Zak."

"It's the new look in heroics."

"What are you doing here? Decided to go over old times with me?"

"Nah, just wanted to know if you knew anything about cheese."

"Gouda, Swiss or cheddar?"

"Actually, pepper jack."

"We don't sell cheese at this farm; we are more of fig farmers here. Planning a dinner party?"

"I was attacked by cheese locusts yesterday, and they were controlled by the wind."

"Zak, Zak , Zak…. I never used dairy products to fight my battles; I stuck with the raw elements." He waves his hands and a gust of wind starts.

"What are you doing?"

He does not answer, and I feel the wind getting stronger and stronger. Trapped under the net, I reach for my communicator to get LEO back up and running, but my hand gets caught before I get to the buttons.

"No need to worry, Zak." The wind lifts the net over my head. "I told you I am a changed man; I have learned my ways to be a proper citizen."

"Yeah, about that… Thanks and sorry."

"No problem, Ranger," he says in a sarcastic tone.

"Let's stick with Zak" I tell him.

CHAPTER TWENTY THREE

Professor Raine is sitting in his laboratory, wearing earphones and playing with a tuner.

"Ha-ha-ha! Stupid Zak Raven. He doesn't realize there is a microphone in the cheese wheel I gave him today. I will soon know all his secrets and use them against him.

A cheese locust flies by him and he shoos it away with his hand. "Darn bugs." He takes off a shoe and smashes the bug against the wall. He takes a cracker from a box and wipes the cheese from his shoe onto the cracker and eats it.

"Mmmmm, tasty. How could Zak Raven be so lame, thinking it was the wind that controlled these bugs? It was the wind from the propellers I set up in the mountains of Bluffside. Which reminds me; I never got a credit slip for the ones I never used."

CHAPTER TWENTY FOUR

"OK, so that lead stunk, Brady." I am riding down the street on the motorcycle, LEO flying behind me. Brady is using some bio lingo that I don't understand through my communicator. "Come on, use English, Brady."

"There is a molecule in the cheese that does not make sense."

"What are you saying?"

"I'm saying that I think I made a mistake in feeding the cheese to the school."

"How bad can it be, Brady? Maybe all it will do is give people gas." I hear a slam at the other end of the communicator. "Brady, what's going on? What was that sound?"

"Zak, we are in trouble. There is a fizz cutting the transmission between us."

I get to the school and it is deserted, which makes sense since it is five p.m. and school let out three hours ago. I park my bike and run to Brady's office. "LEO, secure the perimeter and look for anything unusual."

"Yes, Zak," LEO sputters.

"Not that a flying robot is usual," I say under my breath. I get to Brady's classroom. The windows are knocked out. "LEO, you have anything?"

"Yes, Zak, there is wreckage all over the school. Fifty-two windows have been broken and no human life is around."

"Keep looking for people." I try opening the door to Brady's classroom but it's blocked by a bunch of furniture. "Whatever wanted to get in got in through the window. And it looks like it really wanted to get in bad."

I call out Brady's name and there is no answer. I hop into the windowpane and sit there looking at the wreckage in the classroom. "I am so going to get blamed for this." Most of the desks are turned over and there's a smell of chemicals stewing in the air. I hit a couple of buttons on my communicator and a little hose pops up, spraying a light mist to protect me from the fumes. I hop down into the classroom. I can smell that awful stench of cheese again.

At Brady's desk, I thumb through his papers and see a word that scares me: NACHOS. This can only mean only one thing: There is a monster looking for tortilla chips. I am in shock.

"Yikes!" A powerful blow knocks me to the other side of the classroom. I tumble into a bunch of tables. My wrist communicator is making noises. I hit a couple of buttons and nothing happens. It's shorting out. I pick myself up and feel stickiness on the side where I was hit. More cheese. Gross.

I look for the cheese monster, but he is nowhere to be seen.

"Here cheesy, cheesy monster! Come out, cheesy monster!"

I hear nothing; I pray that the infrared radar works on my communicator. I hit a button and nothing. Upset, I slam my wrist down on desk and the radar goes on.

"Ah, the finest technology." I scan the room and nothing registers but some cheese residue. I scan the floor and I pick up cheese footprints going out the door.

"At least this makes my job easier," I mumble and follow the cheese prints on the floor to where they stop at the janitor's basement. The door is ripped off. I walk down the stairs to the basement. There are a bunch of tools, mops and cheese. There is a door that leads to a bunch of hallways beneath the school, left from the previous school building, which was never completely torn down.

I follow the footsteps of cheese and their smell. I get to what looks like an old auditorium and see what I have been searching for: hundreds of cheese people. Brady is chained to a fence and looks wiped out.

"This is not going to be easy," I think to myself.

I have two choices: 1. Storm in; and 2. Storm in. So I storm in and a bunch of cheese people turn around and shoot cheese sauce from their arms.

I dodge the spray of cheese and do flips over the monsters.

I kick a couple of them and they fall to the floor. At least they are not ninja cheese monsters. Brady gathers some energy and wakes up a little. I knock a couple more cheese people to the floor.

I grab one from behind and am about to shoot it with a blast of my ray.

"Zak, NO!" Brady calls out to me.

"Huh?" I say, stunned. I feel a thump on the back of my head and everything goes black.

CHAPTER TWENTY FIVE

"Uhhh…." I moan. I feel like I got hit by a truck.

"Zak, wake up."

I am chained to the fence beside Brady. There are about a hundred cheesy-looking monsters lurking around.

"What's going on, Brady?"

"These are your classmates."

"Brady, no these are cheese people."

"Listen to me, the molecule that I found in the cheese is the element that turned them into these things. When I was in my office figuring all of this out, they broke in and grabbed me. Next thing I knew, I was chained to this fence."

"What do they want?"

"What does everyone want? To take over the world."

"One slice at a time."

"Zak, this is no time for your smart tongue," Brady scowls. "The big one there is Principal Montal."

"He looks better this way. The orange color looks good on him."

"Where is LEO?"

"I dunno, I can't contact him because my communicator is shorting out."

"There is an override switch to him. Can you hit the third button from the right?"

"Sure thing." I tap my communicator against the fence, hitting a button. "I think I got it" The grappling hook shoots out and makes this big clanging sound against the fence. A couple of cheese monsters look at me. I start to cough. "I have a cold," I say and they go back to what they are doing.

"I'll try it again." I slam it again and nothing happens, then a light flashes. "I think I got it."

"I just hope that LEO will be able to retrieve the location this far under the ground."

"I'll second that."

"So if we do break free from this, how do we stop it?"

"In my office, in the desk, there is an antidote. They did not know that I had it before they took me."

"Hey, since I am here with you and not studying, and if we get out of this alive, can I make up tomorrow's test?"

"No, Zak."

After a while, the cheese monsters get restless. They start some sort of routine where they merge together, and with each merge the one in the middle is getting bigger and bigger.

I'm stunned and ask Brady, "What is going on?"

"They are combining into a giant being."

"Neat."

"I do not know if that qualifies as neat."

"Shhh," I tell Brady. "Do you hear that?"

"Yes."

"The cavalry is here."

LEO floats in. The cheese people are too busy with their ritual to notice him. LEO makes it over to me and floats in front of my face. "Hello, Zak."

"Blast the chains, LEO." That said, LEO's eye starts to get bright and breaks the chains on both Brady and me. "OK, what's the plan Brady?"

"I will distract them and you go for the enzyme antidote."

Brady runs to the other side of the fence and starts yelling. The creatures don't move.

"You are going to have to do better than that!" I yell. "Flap your arms and cluck like a chicken!"

"You're insane," he tells me.

"Try it; what do you have to lose?"

"My dignity," he howls and flaps his arms up and down. If this were not a life or death situation, it would be really funny.

The cheese people notice Brady is not chained to the fence. I grab LEO really tight, telling him to blast off, and we soar above the cheese monsters. They are confused and do not know whether to follow me or go after Brady.

I am sweeping through the halls of the school and holding LEO for dear life. He is going really fast to Brady's office. It is like he has a homing device to the science room. I drop to the ground and run inside to find the serum. I'm going through his desk, searching for what looks like a vile of liquid or something that would be an antidote

"Hmmm… Look what I found, the grade book." I hold this in my hand and think how nice it would be to change all the C's to A's. Then reality hits when a big chunk of cheese flies at my head.

"Mr. Raven, you will come with me now." The big cheeseman does not look familiar but his voice sure does.

"Principal Montal, is that you?" I look down in the desk drawer and find the vile of antidote. I have to be careful not to jeopardize breaking it. I could not go through life with Torrance as my cheese bride. Anyway, she is allergic to cheese. I slowly reach into the drawer while looking at my so-called principal who is now a dairy product.

"So, a question for ya: When you get sick now, are you phlegmy or are you always phlegmy?"

"Groarrrrrrrr!" he roars, shattering the couple of windows in the room that were left.

"I'm guessing that's a bad question to ask ya at this time. What about crackers? Are you a fan of the whole wheat ones? What do you spread on them, because cheese would be kinda cannibalistic, don't you think?" I grab the vile just as he shoots a massive cheese wave at me. Jumping over the desk and bolting through his legs, I run out the door. The only problem is he grabbed my leg.

"I was kidding, no hard feelings?" I'm panicking.

"Groarrrrr," he howls again.

His free hand is pointed down at me, ready to fire when LEO pops in front of him.

"OK, LEO! Let's have some grilled cheese!"

LEO's eyes glow a vibrant red I haven't seen before and blasts the monster to the back of the wall. Principal Cheese is now a bubbling mass of yuck.

"Thanks, buddy." I shake the residue of his hand off my leg and run back to where Brady is.

He's surrounded by a bunch of the monsters.

"I got it, Brady!"

"Finally! Now put it in LEO's side compartment."

"Gotcha."

"And hurry, Zak."

I open LEO's side compartment and insert the vile into him. Nothing happens.

"Now what?" I yell to Brady.

"Push the five four seven eight code on your wrist communicator; it will set off the charge." I can tell he is freaking out as the monsters get within inches of him. "When you hit 'enter,' cover your eyes."

I push the code, hit the enter button and nothing happens. I try it again, still nothing.

"Zak, hurry!"

"I'm trying! Come on, you stupid thing." I slam the wrist communicator against the wall and it starts the five-second countdown. "It's going now, Brady."

"Cover your eyes!" A big blast of light fills the ground where the monsters are standing. I wish I could tell you more of what happened afterward, but since my eyes where closed, I can't. All I know is that before the light went on, there were monsters and after the blast there was nothing but my fellow students covered in cheese.

"Oh, god, my hair." I see Ciara covered in cheese.

There is a shadow figure lurking in the halls. A pair of eyes are looking at me and making me feel uncomfortable. I race toward it to find it was just my imagination.

"That darn kid, one day he will be gone from this town once and for all." Professor Raine gets into his car and drives out of the school parking lot.

EPILOGUE

A week has passed since the school was turned to cheese and everything is back to normal. The halls still have a faint odor of cheese.

I walk into the dance with Tyler and we see Ciara right away. She is wearing a black dress covered with little pink and red roses. It is weird to see her so dressed up. Most of the time people at school wear jeans and T-shirts. Tyler looks nervous.

"If I had a quarter for every time I saw her wearing a dress, I would be flat broke," Tyler laughs. "But she looks really fab."

A slow song starts and the mood in the gym suddenly changes. Most of the kids separate to opposite sides of the gym, boys on one side and girls on the other. Why don't we just go up and ask them to dance, what is the big deal? Then I see Torrance and remember what the big deal is: Rejection bad. Fruit punch good. We walk to the bleachers and sit down. Tyler sits next to me and we talk about nothing. Ciara walks by and glares at me, which to me means WHY HAVEN'T YOU ARRANGED FOR ME TO DANCE WITH TYLER? YOU WILL NEVER COPY ANY HOMEWORK FROM ME AGAIN.

"Ciara, wait," I call out, catching her by surprise.

"Yes?" she says very softly.

"I was thinking about what you said today. You know, about the dance."

She is looking at me like she is going to kill me. "Uh, what do you mean?"

"That you really were hoping that they played good music."

"Oh, yeah, that." Ciara looks relieved.

"I think the music is great, too," Tyler speaks up. I could not have planned it better.

"This is my favorite song," Ciara says.

"Uhhhh, ummm, would you like to dance?"

"I guess so." Ciara smiles and they walk off to the dance floor. I am left alone in the bleachers with the punch and the other guys.

Colton walks by me and for the first time does not say anything. I guess he has changed since I saved Torrance.

I watch my friends dance and am really happy for them. I get up to go outside. At this point, all I want to hear is Torrance yelling my name, asking me to dance, but all I hear is the quietness of a small town. I walk down the street, listening to the crickets chirp. Life is good. I feel like things can only get better from here.

The end for now...

ALSO AVAILABLE FROM MARKOSIA

SINBAD: ROGUE OF MARS

A prophecy foretells of a stranger from distant lands who will vanquish the false king. Eight years after the assassination of King Dadgar, his vile nephew, Adhkar, has usurped his throne and enslaved the Azurian people, igniting a violent civil war. Having sailed the seven seas, exploring unknown lands, fighting countless monsters and battling evil wizards, could Sinbad be the stranger of the prophecy, or will he merely be a pawn in Adhkar's bloody game?

ISBN: 978-1-911243-63-2